This book belongs to

....

Nursery Treasury

Miles Kelly

First published in 2016 by Miles Kelly Publishing Ltd
Harding's Barn, Bardfield End Green, Thaxted, Essex, CM6 3PX, UK

Copyright © Miles Kelly Publishing Ltd 2016

2 4 6 8 10 9 7 5 3 1

Publishing Director Belinda Gallagher
Creative Director Jo Cowan
Editorial Director Rosie Neave
Editors Fran Bromage, Claire Philip
Designers Jo Cowan, Joe Jones
Production Elizabeth Collins, Caroline Kelly
Reprographics Stephan Davis, Jennifer Cozens, Thom Allaway
Assets Lorraine King

ISBN 978-1-78617-039-2

Printed in China

British Library Cataloguing-in-Publication Data
A catalogue record for this book is available from the British Library

ACKNOWLEDGEMENTS
The publishers would like to thank Sanja Rescek (The Bright Agency) for the cover artwork
All other artwork from the Miles Kelly Artwork Bank

Made with paper from a sustainable forest

www.mileskelly.net

CONTENTS

BEST-LOVED RHYMES

FAVOURITE FOLK

ANIMAL FRIENDS

PLAYING TOGETHER

TASTY TREATS

OUT AND ABOUT

NUMBER RHYMES

WHATEVER THE WEATHER

BEDTIME RHYMES

STORY TIME

BEST-LOVED RHYMES

Have you any wool?

Oh, the grand old Duke of York

Old Macdonald had a Farm

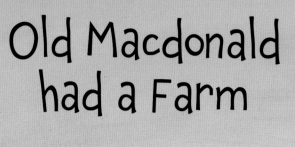

Old Macdonald had a farm,
E-I-E-I-O!
And on that farm he had
some cows, E-I-E-I-O!
With a moo-moo here,
And a moo-moo there,
Here a moo, there a moo,
Everywhere a moo-moo,
Old Macdonald had a farm,
E-I-E-I-O!

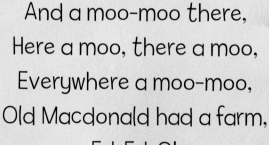

Old Macdonald had a farm, E-I-E-I-O!
And on that farm he had some sheep, E-I-E-I-O!
With a baa-baa here,
And a baa-baa there,
Here a baa, there a baa,
Everywhere a baa-baa,
Old Macdonald had a farm, E-I-E-I-O!

Old Macdonald had a farm, E-I-E-I-O!
And on that farm he had some ducks, E-I-E-I-O!
With a quack-quack here,
And a quack-quack there,
Here a quack, there a quack,
Everywhere a quack-quack,
Old Macdonald had a farm,
E-I-E-I-O!

Old Macdonald had a farm, E-I-E-I-O!
And on that farm he had some pigs, E-I-E-I-O!
With an oink-oink here,
And an oink-oink there,
Here an oink, there an oink,
Everywhere an oink-oink,
Old Macdonald had a farm, E-I-E-I-O!

Humpty Dumpty

Humpty Dumpty sat on a wall,
Humpty Dumpty had a great fall;
All the king's horses
and all the king's men
Couldn't put Humpty
together again.

See-saw, Margery Daw

See-saw, Margery Daw,
Johnny shall have a new master;
He shall have but a penny a day,
Because he can't work any faster.

Little Miss Muffet

Little Miss Muffet
Sat on a tuffet,
Eating her curds and whey;
Along came a spider,
Who sat down beside her,
And frightened Miss Muffet away.

Pat-a-Cake

Pat-a-cake, pat-a-cake, baker's man,
Bake me a cake as fast as you can.
Pat it and prick it, and mark it with 'B',
And put it in the oven
For Baby and me.

Baa, Baa, Black Sheep

Baa, baa, black sheep,
Have you any wool?
Yes, sir, yes, sir,
Three bags full:
One for the master,
And one for the dame,
And one for the little boy
Who lives down the lane.

Mary's Lamb

Mary had a little lamb,
Its fleece was white as snow;
And everywhere that Mary went
The lamb was sure to go.

It followed her to school one day,
That was against the rules.
It made the children laugh and play,
To see a lamb at school.

Jack and Jill

Jack and Jill went up the hill
To fetch a pail of water;
Jack fell down and broke his crown,
And Jill came tumbling after.

Up Jack got, and home did trot,
As fast as he could caper.
He went to bed,
To mend his head
With vinegar and brown paper.

Hickory, Dickory, Dock

Hickory, dickory, dock!
The mouse ran up the clock.
The clock struck one,
The mouse ran down,
Hickory, dickory, dock!

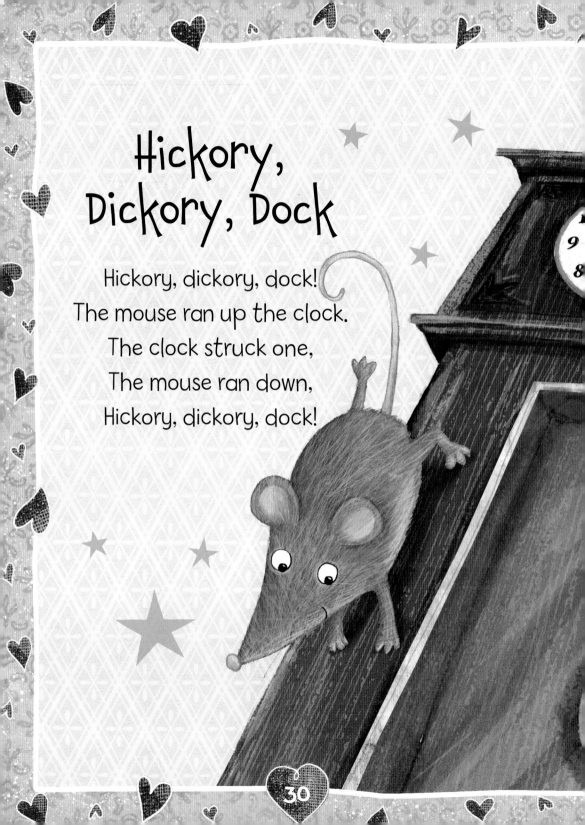

Hickory, dickory, dock!
The mouse ran up the clock.
The clock struck two,
The mouse said, "Boo!"
Hickory, dickory, dock.

Hickory, dickory, dock!
The mouse ran up the clock.
The clock struck three,
The mouse said, "Weeee!"
Hickory, dickory, dock.

Hickory, dickory, dock!
The mouse ran up the clock.
The clock struck four,
Let's sing some more!
Hickory, dickory, dock.

Hey Diddle Diddle

Hey diddle diddle,
The cat and the fiddle,
The cow jumped over the moon;
The little dog laughed
To see such fun,
And the dish ran away with the spoon.

Duke of York

Oh, the grand old Duke of York,
He had ten thousand men;
He marched them up to the top of the hill,
And he marched them down again.

And when they were up, they were up,
And when they were down, they were down.
And when they were only halfway up,
They were neither up nor down.

Little Bo-Peep

Little Bo-Peep has lost her sheep,
And doesn't know where to find them;

Leave them alone
and they'll come home,
Bringing their tails
behind them.

Monday's Child

Monday's child is
fair of face,

Tuesday's child is
full of grace,

Wednesday's child is
full of woe,

Thursday's child has
far to go,

Friday's child is
loving and giving,

Saturday's child works
hard for a living,

But the child that is born
on the Sabbath day,
Is bonny and blithe
and good and gay.

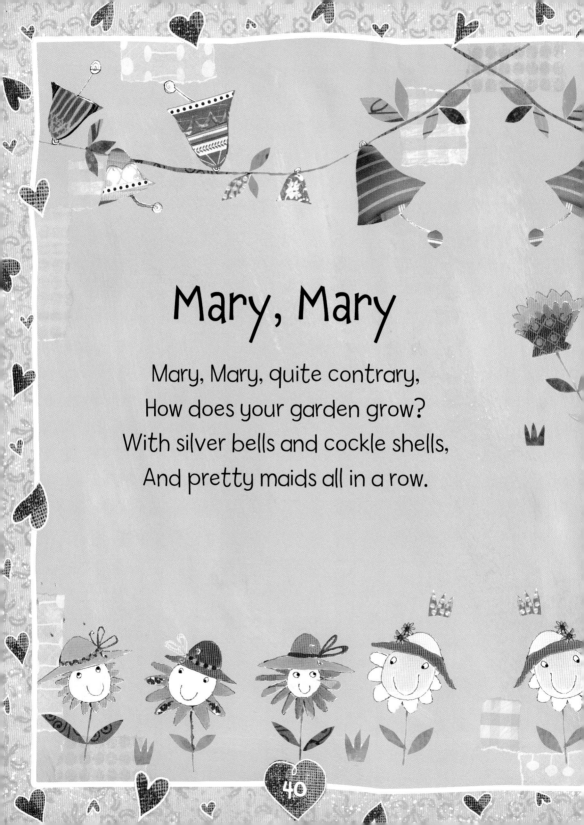

Mary, Mary

Mary, Mary, quite contrary,
How does your garden grow?
With silver bells and cockle shells,
And pretty maids all in a row.

Polly, put the kettle on

Polly, put the kettle on,
Polly, put the kettle on,
Polly, put the kettle on,
We'll all have tea.

Sukey, take it off again,
Sukey, take it off again,
Sukey, take it off again,
They've all gone away.

42

Bye baby bunting, Father's gone a-hunting

44

FAVOURITE FOLK

Here I am,
Little jumping Joan

There was an Old Man with a beard

Little Boy Blue

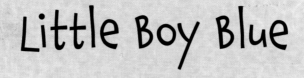

Little Boy Blue,
Come blow your horn,
The sheep's in the meadow,
The cow's in the corn.

But where is the boy
Who looks after the sheep?
He's under a haystack,
Fast asleep!

Will you wake him?
No, not I,
For if I do,
He'll surely cry.

Lucy Locket

Lucy Locket lost her pocket,
Kitty Fisher found it;
Not a penny was there in it,
But a ribbon round it.

49

There was a Crooked Man

There was a crooked man,
And he walked a crooked mile,
He found a crooked sixpence
Upon a crooked stile;
He bought a crooked cat,
Which caught a crooked mouse,
And they all lived together
In a little crooked house.

The Old Woman who Lived in a Shoe

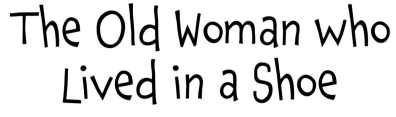

There was an old woman
who lived in a shoe,
She had so many children
she didn't know what to do.
She gave them some broth
without any bread,

Then told them all
off and sent them
to bed.

Curly Locks

Curly Locks, Curly Locks,
Wilt thou be mine?
Thou shalt not wash dishes,
Nor yet feed the swine;

But sit on a cushion,
And sew a fine seam,
And feed upon strawberries,
Sugar and cream.

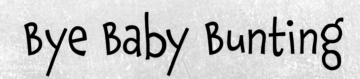

Bye Baby Bunting

Bye baby bunting,
Father's gone a-hunting,
To get a little rabbit skin,
To wrap his little baby in.

Little Girl, Little Girl

Little girl, little girl,
Where have you been?
Gathering roses
To give to the queen.

Little girl, little girl,
What gave she you?
She gave me a diamond
As big as my shoe.

There was an Old Man

There was an Old Man with a beard,
Who said, "It is just as I feared!
Two Owls and a Hen,
Four Larks and a Wren,
Have all built their nests
in my beard."

Edward Lear
1812–88, b. England

O Dear, what can the Matter be?

O dear, what can the matter be?
Dear, dear, what can the matter be?
O dear, what can the matter be?
Johnny's so long at the fair.

He promised to bring me a basket of posies,
A garland of lilies, a garland of roses,
A little straw hat, to set off the ribbons
That tie up my bonny brown hair.

Jumping Joan

Here I am,
Little jumping Joan;
When nobody's with me
I'm all alone.

Here is the Church

Here is the church,
And here is the steeple,
Open the door and see all the people.
Here is the parson going upstairs,
And here he is saying his prayers.

Father's Day

"Walk a little slower, Daddy,"
said a child so small.
"I'm following in your footsteps
and I don't want to fall.

Sometimes your steps are very fast,
Sometimes they're hard to see;
So, walk a little slower, Daddy,
For you are leading me.

Someday when I'm all grown up,
You're what I want to be;
Then I will have a little child
Who'll want to follow me.

And I would want to lead just right,
And know that I was true;
So walk a little slower, Daddy,
For I must follow you."

Author unknown

Jack be Nimble

Jack be nimble,
Jack be quick,
Jack jump over the candlestick.

Lavender's Blue

Lavender's blue, dilly, dilly,
Lavender's green,
When I am King, dilly, dilly,
You shall be Queen.

Who told you so, dilly, dilly,
Who told you so?
'Twas my own heart, dilly, dilly,
That told me so.

Call up your men, dilly, dilly,
Set them to work,
Some to the plough, dilly, dilly,
Some to the cart.

Some to make hay, dilly, dilly,
Some to make corn,
While you and I, dilly, dilly
Keep ourselves warm.

Lavender's green, dilly, dilly,
Lavender's blue,
If you love me, dilly, dilly,
I will love you.

Little Polly Flinders

Little Polly Flinders
Sat among the cinders,
Warming her pretty little toes.

Her mother came and caught her,
And told off her little daughter
For spoiling her nice new clothes.

Old King Cole

Old King Cole was a merry old soul,
And a merry old soul was he;
He called for his pipe,
And he called for his bowl,
And he called for his fiddlers three.

Every fiddler had a fine fiddle,
And a very fine fiddle had he.
Oh, there's none so rare,
As can compare
With King Cole and his fiddlers three!

There was a Little Girl

There was a little girl, and she had a little curl,
Right in the middle of her forehead;
When she was good, she was very, very good,
But when she was bad, she was horrid!

Dance to your Daddy

Dance to your daddy,
My bonnie laddy,
Dance to your daddy,
My bonnie lamb.

You shall have a fishy,
In a little dishy,
You shall have a fishy,
When the boat comes in.

Dance to your daddy,
My bonnie laddy,
Dance to your daddy,
And to your mammy sing.

You shall get a coatie,
And a pair of breekies,
You shall get a coatie,
When the boat comes in.

There was an Old Woman

There was an old woman
Tossed up in a basket,
Seventeen times as high as the moon.
Where she was going
I just had to ask it,
For in her hand she carried a broom.

"Old woman, old woman, old woman," said I,
"O whither, O whither, O whither so high?"
"To sweep the cobwebs off the sky!
And I'll be with you
By and by."

I've been to London,
To visit the queen

ANIMAL FRIENDS

She wanders lowing here and there

So whene'er you meet a crocodile

What does the Bee do?

What does the bee do?
Bring home honey.
And what does Father do?
Bring home money.
And what does Mother do?
Lay out the money.
And what does baby do?
Eat up the honey.

Christina Rossetti
1830–94, b. England

Goosey, Goosey Gander

Goosey, goosey gander,
Whither shall I wander?
Upstairs and downstairs
And in my lady's chamber.

There I met an old man
Who would not say his prayers;
So I took him by his left leg
And threw him down the stairs.

Cock-a-Doodle-Doo

Cock-a-doodle-doo!
My dame has lost her shoe,
My master's lost his fiddling stick,
And doesn't know what to do.

Cock-a-doodle-doo!
My dame has found her shoe,
My master's found his fiddling stick,
So cock-a-doodle-do!

Little Robin Redbreast

Little Robin Redbreast sat upon a tree,
Up went pussy cat, and down went he!
Down came pussy cat, and away Robin ran;
Says little Robin Redbreast, "Catch me if you can!"

Little Robin Redbreast jumped upon a spade,
Pussy cat jumped after him,
and then he was afraid.
Little Robin chirped and sang,
and what did Pussy say?
Pussy cat said, "Mew, mew, mew,"
and Robin jumped away.

Little Robin Redbreast jumped upon a wall,
Pussy cat jumped after him,
and almost got a fall!
Little Robin chirped and sang,
and what did Pussy say?
Pussy cat said, "Mew," and Robin flew away.

A Cat came Fiddling

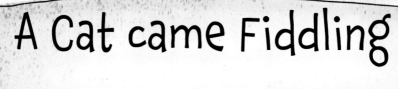

A cat came fiddling out of a barn,
With a pair of bagpipes under her arm.
She could sing nothing but fiddle dee dee,
The mouse has married the bumblebee.
Pipe, cat; dance, mouse;
We'll have a wedding at our good house.

Ducks' Ditty

All along the backwater,
Through the rushes tall,
Ducks are a-dabbling.
Up tails all!

Ducks' tails, drakes' tails,
Yellow feet a-quiver,
Yellow bills all out of sight
Busy in the river!

Slushy green undergrowth
Where the roach swim
Here we keep our larder,
Cool and full and dim.

Everyone for what he likes!
We like to be
Heads down, tails up,
Dabbling free!

High in the blue above
Swifts whirl and call
We are down a-dabbling
Up tails all!

Kenneth Grahame
1859–1932, b. Scotland

The Cow

The friendly cow all red and white,
I love with all my heart.
She gives me cream with all her might,
To eat with apple tart.
She wanders lowing here and there,
And yet she cannot stray,
All in the pleasant open air,
The pleasant light of day;
And blown by all the winds that pass
And wet with all the showers,
She walks among the meadow grass
And eats the meadow flowers.

Robert Louis Stevenson
1850–94, b. Scotland

Pussy Cat Mole

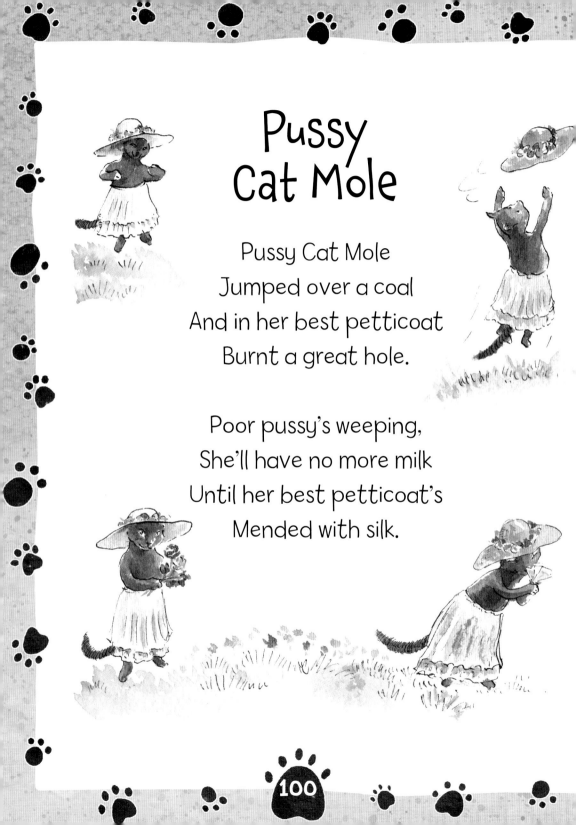

Pussy Cat Mole
Jumped over a coal
And in her best petticoat
Burnt a great hole.

Poor pussy's weeping,
She'll have no more milk
Until her best petticoat's
Mended with silk.

High in the Pine Tree

High in the pine tree,
The little turtledove
Made a little nursery
To please her little love.

"Coo," said the turtledove,
"Coo," said she,
In the long shady branches
Of the dark pine tree.

Where, O Where

Where, O where,
Has my little dog gone?
O where, O where, can he be?
With his tail cut short,
And his ears cut long,
O where, O where, has he gone?

I Love Little Pussy

I love little pussy,
Her coat is so warm,
And if I don't hurt her,
She'll do me no harm.

So I'll not pull her tail,
Nor drive her away,
But pussy and I,
Very gently will play.

I'll sit by the fire,
And give her some food;
And pussy will love me
Because I am good.

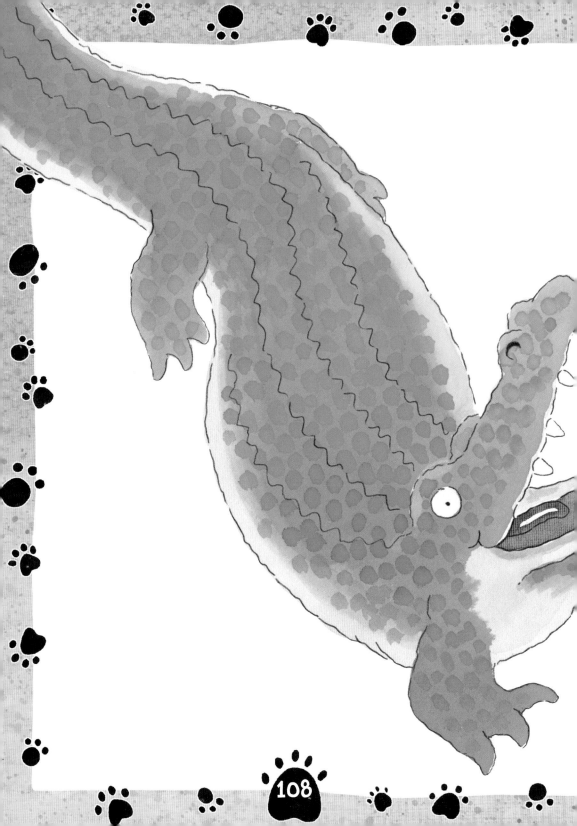

The Crocodile

If you should meet a crocodile
Don't take a stick and poke him;
Ignore the welcome in his smile,
Be careful not to stroke him.

For as he sleeps upon the Nile,
He thinner gets and thinner;
So whene'er you meet a crocodile
He's ready for his dinner.

Christine F Fletcher

Who killed Cock Robin?

Who killed Cock Robin?
"I," said the Sparrow,
"With my bow and arrow,
I killed Cock Robin."

Who saw him die?
"I," said the Fly,
"With my little eye,
I saw him die."

Who caught his blood?
"I," said the Fish,
"With my little dish,
I caught his blood."

Who'll dig his grave?
"I," said the Owl,
"With my spade and trowel,
I'll dig his grave."

Who'll be the clerk?
"I," said the Lark,
"If it's not in the dark,
I'll be the clerk."

Who'll be the parson?
"I," said the Rook,
"With my little book,
I'll be the parson."

Who'll sing a psalm?
"I," said the Thrush,
As she sat on a bush,
"I'll sing a psalm."

Who'll be chief mourner?
"I," said the Dove,
"I mourn for my love,
I'll be chief mourner."

Who'll toll the bell?
"I," said the Bull,
"Because I can pull,
I'll toll the bell."

All the birds of the air
Fell sighing and sobbing,
When they heard the bell toll
For poor Cock Robin.

Pussy Cat, Pussy Cat

Pussy cat, pussy cat,
Where have you been?
I've been to London,
To visit the queen.
Pussy cat, pussy cat,
What did you there?
I frightened a
little mouse,
Under her chair.

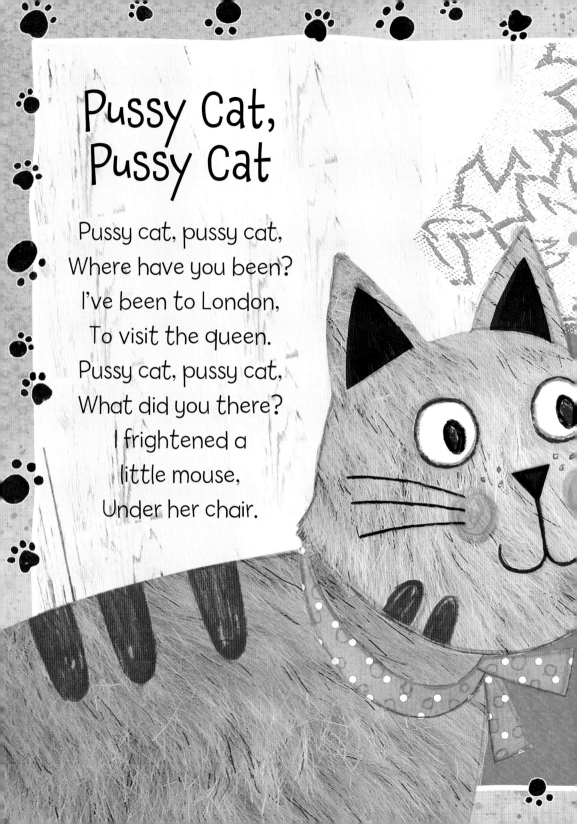

The Hobby-horse

I had a little hobby-horse,
And it was dapple grey;
Its head was made of pea-straw,
Its tail was made of hay.

I sold it to an old woman
For a copper groat;
And I'll not sing my song again
Without another coat.

The Lion and the Unicorn

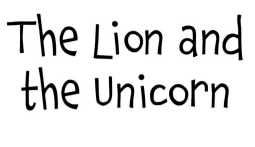

The lion and the unicorn
Were fighting for the crown;
The lion beat the unicorn
All around the town.

Some gave them white bread
And some gave them brown;
Some gave them plum cake
And drummed them out of town!

The Little Turtle

There was a little turtle,
He lived in a box.
He swam in a puddle,
He climbed on the rocks.

He snapped at a mosquito,
He snapped at a flea.
He snapped at a minnow,
And he snapped at me.

He caught the mosquito,
He caught the flea.
He caught the minnow,
But he didn't catch me.

Vachel Lindsay
1879–1931, b. USA

Ding, Dong, Bell

Ding, dong, bell,
Pussy's in the well.

Who put her in?
Little Johnny Flynn.

Who pulled her out?
Little Tommy Stout.

What a naughty boy was that
To try to drown poor pussy cat,

Who never did him any harm,
But killed the mice in the farmer's barn.

Gently down
the stream

PLAYING TOGETHER

Beep, beep, beep! Beep, beep, beep!

One potato, Two potato

Ring-a-ring o' Roses

Ring-a-ring o' roses,
A pocket full of posies,
A-tishoo! A-tishoo!
We all fall down.

All hold hands and skip round
in a ring. As you say the last line, all
sit down on the ground, then repeat.

The king has sent his daughter,
To fetch a pail of water,
A-tishoo! A-tishoo!
We all fall down.

The bird upon the steeple,
Sits high above the people,
A-tishoo! A-tishoo!
We all fall down.

Five Little Peas

Five little peas
In a peapod pressed,
One grew, two grew,
And so did all the rest.
They grew and grew
And did not stop,
Until one day
The peapod popped!

Curl one hand into a fist. As you say
the rhyme, pop out one finger, then a
thumb and then all the rest. Spread
your arms out and clap at the end.

If you're Happy and you Know it

If you're happy and you know it,
clap your hands.
If you're happy and you know it,
clap your hands.
If you're happy and you know it
and you really want to show it,
If you're happy and you know it,
clap your hands.

Clap your hands when you get to those words in the rhyme.

Stamp your feet when you get to those
words in the rhyme, then nod your head
when you reach the third verse.

If you're happy and you know it,
stamp your feet.
If you're happy and you know it,
stamp your feet.
If you're happy and you know it
and you really want to show it,
If you're happy and you know it,
stamp your feet.

If you're happy and you know it,
nod your head.
If you're happy and you know it,
nod your head.
If you're happy and you know it
and you really want to show it,
If you're happy and you know it,
nod your head.

Row, Row, Row
your Boat

Row, row, row your boat,
Gently down the stream.
Merrily, merrily, merrily, merrily,
Life is but a dream.

Row, row, row your boat,
Gently down the stream.
If you see a crocodile,
Don't forget to scream!

Row, row, row your boat,
Gently to the shore.
If you see a lion,
Don't forget to roar!

Sit across from your
partner, holding hands and
rocking back and forth.
Scream on the second verse!
Roar on the third verse!

Round and Round the Garden

Round and round the garden
Like a teddy bear,
One step, two step,
Tickle you under there!

Draw circles with your finger around
the palm. Walk your fingers up the arm
in two steps. Tickle under the arm!

One Potato

One potato,
Two potato,
Three potato,
Four,
Five potato,
Six potato,
Seven potato more.

Take turns with your partner in placing one fist on top of another to build a tower.

When you reach seven start again.

I'm a Little Teapot

I'm a little teapot,
Short and stout,
Here's my handle,
Here's my spout.

When I see the teacups,
Hear me shout,
"Tip me up, and pour me out!"

Place one hand on your
hip to be the handle.

Place the other arm out to
the side to be the spout.

On the final line, lean over to
one side to pour the tea.

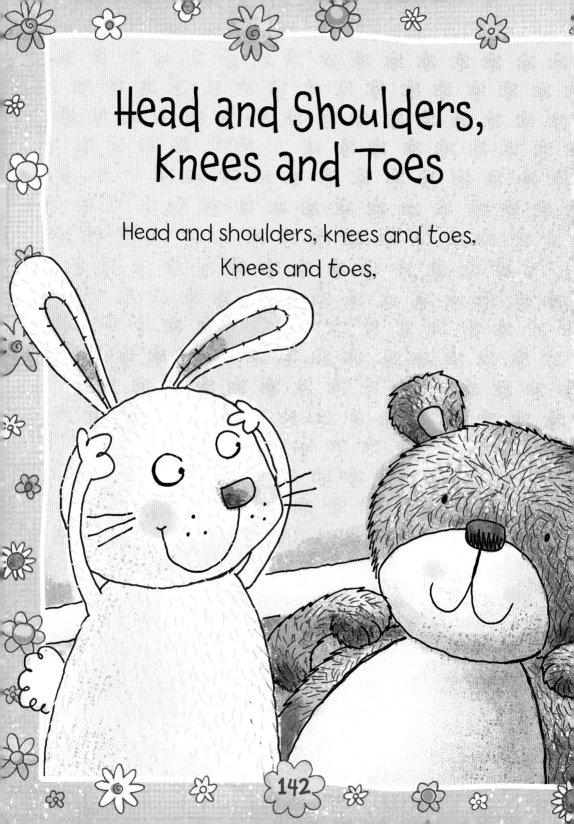

Head and Shoulders, Knees and Toes

Head and shoulders, knees and toes,
Knees and toes,

Head and shoulders, knees and toes,
Knees and toes,

And eyes and ears and mouth and nose,

Head and shoulders, knees and toes,
Knees and toes.

Touch each part of
the body as you
sing the rhyme.

One, Two, Three, Four, Five

One, two, three, four, five,
Once I caught a fish alive;
Six, seven, eight, nine, ten,
Then I let it go again.

Why did you let it go?
Because it bit my finger so.
Which finger did it bite?
This little finger on my right.

Count to five using your fingers on
one hand, then count to ten using the
other hand. Shake out both hands.

Pretend to bite, then wiggle your
little finger on the right hand.

This Little Pig

This little pig went to market;

Market

This little pig stayed at home;
This little pig had roast beef;
This little pig had none;

Read the first line and
wiggle the big toe.
Read the next line and wiggle
the next toe and so on. On
the final line, tickle the foot.

The Wheels on the Bus

The wheels on the bus
go round and round,
Round and round, round and round.
The wheels on the bus
go round and round,
All day long.
(Roll your hands over each other.)

The horn on the bus
goes beep, beep, beep!
Beep, beep, beep! Beep, beep, beep!
The horn on the bus
goes beep, beep, beep!
All day long.
(Pretend to honk the horn.)

The wipers on the bus go swish, swish, swish!
Swish, swish, swish! Swish, swish, swish!
The wipers on the bus go swish, swish, swish!
All day long.
(Swish your arms like windscreen wipers.)

The people on the bus bounce up and down,
Up and down, up and down.
The people on the bus
bounce up and down,
All day long.
(Bounce up and down.)

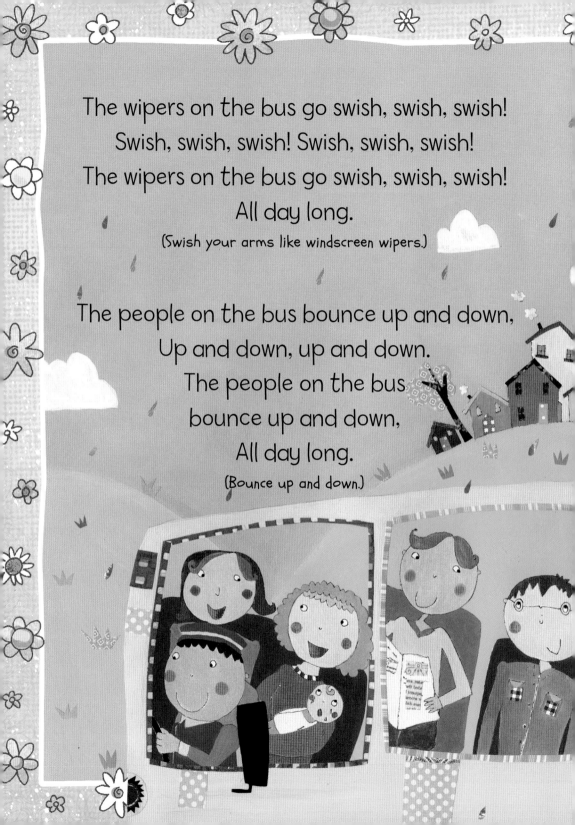

The mummies on the bus
go chatter, chatter, chatter,
Chatter, chatter, chatter!
Chatter, chatter, chatter!
The mummies on the bus
go chatter, chatter, chatter!
All day long.

(Open and close your fingers and thumb.)

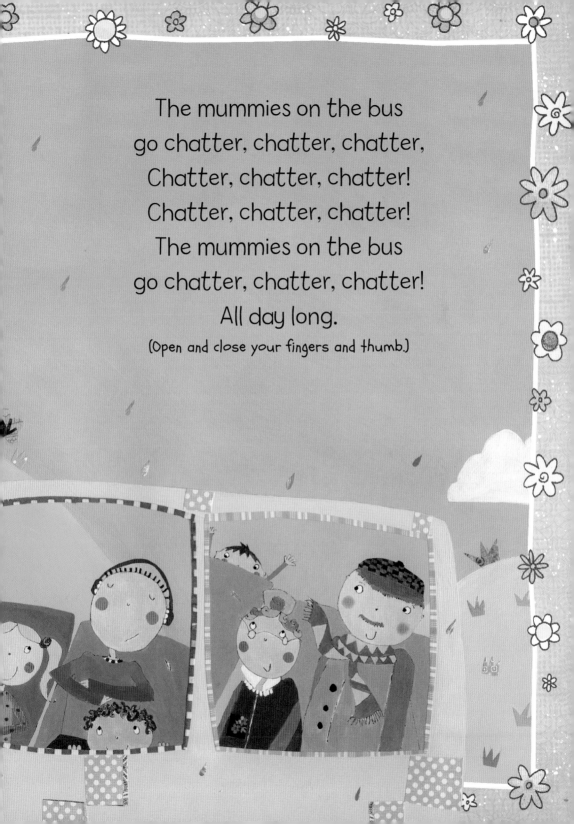

Two Little Dicky birds

Two little dicky birds sitting on a wall;
One named Peter, one named Paul.
Fly away Peter, fly away Paul!
Come back Peter, come back Paul!

Use your index fingers
to be Peter and Paul.

Wiggle each finger in turn.

Next, put each finger behind
you as if to fly away.

On the last line, bring each
finger back in front of you.

I Hear Thunder

I hear thunder, I hear thunder,
Hark, don't you?
Hark, don't you?
Pitter patter raindrops,
Pitter patter raindrops,
I'm wet through,
So are you.

Crash!

Boom!

Cup one hand to your ear.

Use both hands to wiggle
fingers like rain drops.

Shake your hands as if
you're drying them.

Simple Simon
met a pieman

TASTY TREATS

Kissed the girls and made them cry

They licked the platter clean

The Queen of Hearts

The Queen of Hearts,
She made some tarts,
All on a summer's day;
The Knave of Hearts,
He stole the tarts,
And took them clean away.

The King of Hearts
Called for the tarts,
And beat the Knave full sore;
The Knave of Hearts
Brought back the tarts,
And vowed he'd steal no more.

Peter Piper

Peter Piper picked
a peck of pickled peppers;

A peck of pickled peppers
Peter Piper picked.

If Peter Piper picked
a peck of pickled peppers,

Where's the peck
of pickled peppers
Peter Piper picked?

Georgie Porgie

Georgie Porgie, pudding and pie,
Kissed the girls and made them cry;
When the boys came out to play,
Georgie Porgie ran away.

I had a Little Nut Tree

I had a little nut tree,
Nothing would it bear
But a silver nutmeg
And a golden pear;
The King of Spain's daughter
Came to visit me,
And all for the sake
Of my little nut tree.

Peter, Peter

Peter, Peter, pumpkin eater,
Had a wife and couldn't keep her!
He put her in a pumpkin shell,
And there he kept her very well!

Mix a Pancake

Mix a pancake,
Stir a pancake,
Pop it in the pan;

Fry the pancake;
Toss the pancake,
Catch it if you can.

Christina Rossetti
1830–94, b. England

169

Little Jack Horner

Little Jack Horner
Sat in the corner,
Eating his Christmas pie;
He put in a thumb,
And pulled out a plum,
And said, "What a good boy am I."

I always Eat my Peas with Honey

I always eat my peas with honey;
I've done it all my life.
It makes the peas taste kind of funny
But it keeps them on the knife.

Anonymous

Simple Simon

Simple Simon met a pieman
Going to the fair;
Says Simple Simon to the pieman,
"Let me taste your ware."

Says the pieman to Simple Simon,
"Show me first your penny."
Says Simple Simon to the pieman,
"Sir, I haven't any."

Old Mother Hubbard

Old Mother Hubbard
Went to the cupboard,
To get her poor dog a bone.
But when she got there
The cupboard was bare,
And so the poor dog had none.

What are Little Boys made of?

What are little boys made of?
Frogs and snails, and puppy dogs' tails,
That's what little boys are made of.

What are little girls made of?
Sugar and spice, and all things nice,
That's what little girls are made of.

Little Tommy Tucker

Little Tommy Tucker
Sings for his supper.

What shall we give him?
White bread and butter.

How shall he cut it
Without a knife?

How will he be married
Without a wife?

181

Pease Porridge Hot

Pease porridge hot,
Pease porridge cold,
Pease porridge in the pot,
Nine days old.

Some like it hot,
Some like it cold,
Some like it in the pot,
Nine days old!

Oranges and Lemons

"Oranges and lemons",
Say the bells of St Clement's.

"You owe me five farthings",
Say the bells of St Martin's.

"When will you pay me?"
Say the bells of Old Bailey.

"When I grow rich,"
Say the bells of Shoreditch.

"When will that be?"
Say the bells of Stepney.

"I do not know,"
Says the great bell of Bow.

Here comes a candle to light you to bed.
Here comes a chopper to chop off your head!

Tom, Tom the Piper's Son

Tom, Tom, the piper's son,
Stole a pig, and away did run,
The pig was eat,
And Tom was beat,
And Tom went howling
Down the street.

187

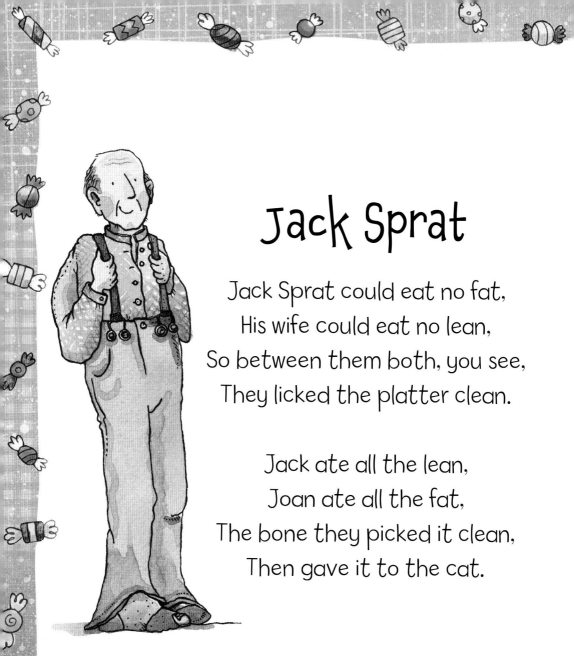

Jack Sprat

Jack Sprat could eat no fat,
His wife could eat no lean,
So between them both, you see,
They licked the platter clean.

Jack ate all the lean,
Joan ate all the fat,
The bone they picked it clean,
Then gave it to the cat.

The Muffin Man

O, do you know the muffin man,
The muffin man, the muffin man,
O, do you know the muffin man,
Who lives in Drury Lane?

O yes, I know the muffin man,
The muffin man, the muffin man,
O yes, I know the muffin man,
Who lives in Drury Lane.

I saw three ships
come sailing by

OUT AND ABOUT

Up and down the City Road,
In and out The Eagle

He'll come back and marry me

Rub-a-dub-dub

Rub-a-dub-dub,
Three men in a tub,
And who do you think they be?
The butcher, the baker,
The candlestick maker,
And all of them going to sea.

Pop goes the weasel

Half a pound of tuppenny rice,
Half a pound of treacle,
That's the way the money goes,
Pop goes the weasel!

Up and down the City Road,
In and out The Eagle,
That's the way the money goes,
Pop goes the weasel!

Every night when I go out
The monkey's on the table,
Take a stick and knock it off,
Pop goes the weasel!

Bobby Shaftoe

Bobby Shaftoe's gone to sea,
Silver buckles on his knee;
He'll come back and marry me,
Bonny Bobby Shaftoe!

Bobby Shaftoe's young and fair,
Combing down his yellow hair;
He's my love for evermore,
Bonny Bobby Shaftoe!

This is the Way

This is the way the ladies ride,
Tri, tre, tre, tree,
Tri, tre, tre, tree,
This is the way the ladies ride,
Tri, tre, tre, tre, tri-tre-tre-tree!

This is the way
the gentlemen ride,
Gallop-a-trip,
Gallop-a-trot,
This is the way
the gentlemen ride,
Gallop-a-gallop-a-trot!

This is the way the farmers ride,
Hobbledy-hoy,
Hobbledy-hoy;
his is the way the farmers ride,
Hobbledy, hobbledy-hoy!

Ladybird, Ladybird

Ladybird, ladybird fly away home,
Your house is on fire
And your children are gone,
All except one and that's little Ann,
For she crept under the frying pan.

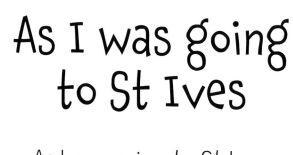

As I was going to St Ives

As I was going to St Ives,
I met a man with seven wives.
Each wife had seven sacks,
Each sack had seven cats,
Each cat had seven kits;
Kits, cats, sacks and wives,
How many were going to St Ives?

If all the World were Paper

If all the world were paper,
And all the sea were ink,
If all the trees were bread and cheese,
What should we have to drink?

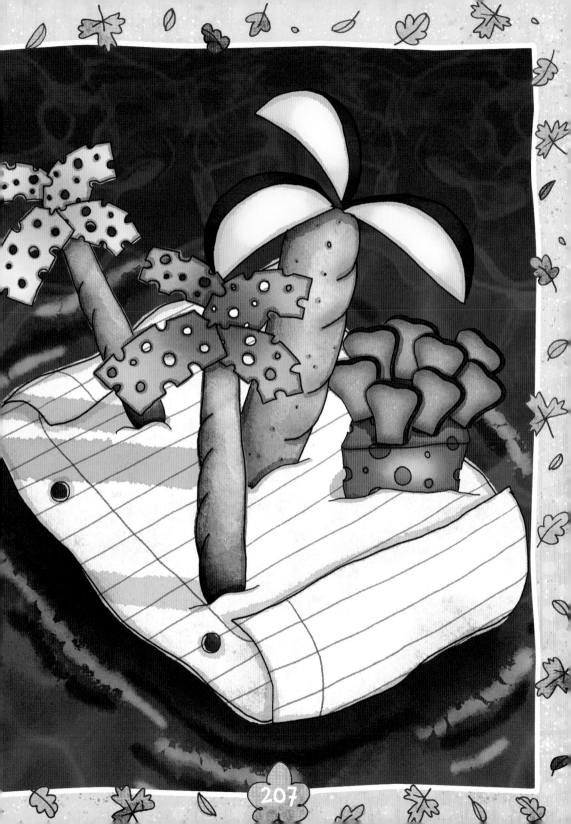

To Market, to Market

To market, to market
to buy a fat pig;
Home again, home again,
jiggety-jig.

To market, to market
to buy a fat hog;
Home again, home again,
jiggety-jog.

Yankee Doodle

Yankee Doodle came to town,
Riding on a pony;
He stuck a feather in his cap
And called it macaroni.

Yankee doodle, doodle do,
Yankee doodle dandy,
All the lasses are so smart,
And sweet as sugar candy.

I Saw Three Ships

I saw three ships come sailing by,
Sailing by, sailing by,
I saw three ships come sailing by,
On New Year's Day in the morning.

And what do you think
was in them then,
In them then,
in them then?
And what do you think
was in them then,
On New Year's Day in
the morning?

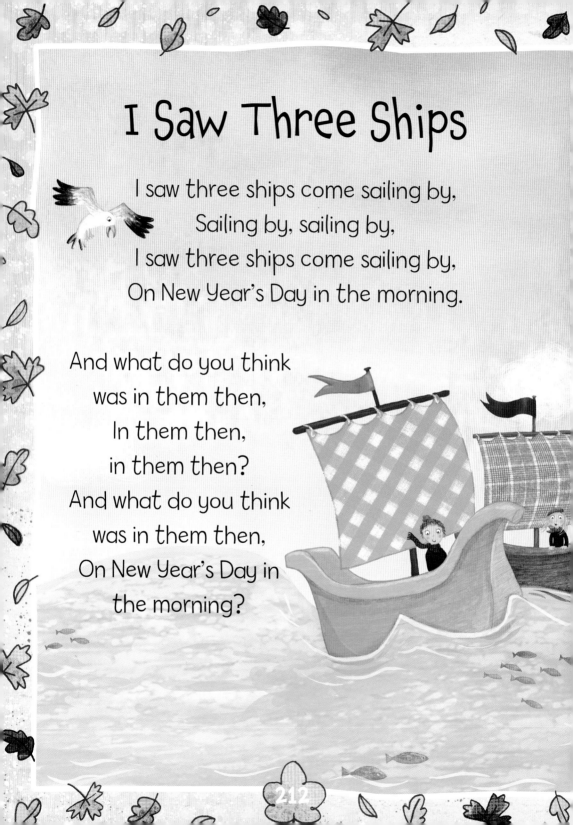

Three pretty girls were in them then,
In them then, in them then,
Three pretty girls were in them then,
On New Year's Day in the morning.

How many Miles to Babylon?

How many miles to Babylon?
Three score miles and ten.
Can I get there by candlelight?
Aye, and back again.
If your feet are nimble and light,
You may get there by candlelight.

As I was Going Out

As I was going out one day
My head fell off and rolled away,
But when I saw that it was gone,
I picked it up and put it on.

And when I got into the street
A fellow cried, "Look at your feet!"
I looked at them and sadly said,
"I've left both asleep in bed!"

Ride a Cock Horse

Ride a cock horse
To Banbury Cross,
To see a fine lady
Upon a white horse.
With rings on her fingers
And bells on her toes,
She shall have music
Wherever she goes.

London Bridge is Falling Down

London Bridge is falling down,
Falling down, falling down,
London Bridge is falling down,
My fair lady.

Build it up with wood and clay,
Wood and clay, wood and clay,
Build it up with wood and clay,
My fair lady.

Wood and clay will wash away,
Wash away, wash away,
Wood and clay will wash away,
My fair lady.

If all the Seas were One Sea

If all the seas were one sea,
What a great sea that would be!
If all the trees were one tree,
What a great tree that would be!

If all the axes were one axe,
What a great axe that would be!
If all the men were one man,
What a great man that would be!

And if the great man took the great axe
And cut down the great tree,
And let it fall into the great sea,
What a great splish-splash that would be!

NUMBER RHYMES

Four-and-twenty blackbirds

Six little mice
sat down to spin

225

Five Little Ducks

Five little ducks went swimming one day,
Over the hill and far away.
Mother duck said,
"Quack, quack, quack, quack!"
But only four little ducks came back.

Four little ducks went swimming one day,
Over the hill and far away.
Mother duck said,
"Quack, quack, quack, quack!"
But only three little ducks came back.

Three little ducks went swimming one day,
Over the hill and far away.
Mother duck said,
"Quack, quack, quack, quack!"
But only two little ducks came back.

Two little ducks went swimming one day,
Over the hill and far away.
Mother duck said,
"Quack, quack, quack, quack!"
But only one little duck came back.

One little duck went swimming one day,
Over the hill and far away.
Mother duck said,
"Quack, quack, quack, quack!"
And all her five little ducks came back!

One, Two, Three, Four

One, two, three, four,
Mary at the kitchen door.
Five, six, seven, eight,
Eating cherries off a plate.

Sing a Song of Sixpence

Sing a song of sixpence,
A pocket full of rye;
Four-and-twenty blackbirds
Baked in a pie.

When the pie was opened,
The birds began to sing;
Wasn't that a dainty dish
To set before the king?

The king was in his counting house,
Counting out his money;
The queen was in the parlour
Eating bread and honey.

The maid was in the garden
Hanging out the clothes,
When down came a blackbird,
And pecked off her nose.

One, Two, Buckle my Shoe

One, two,
buckle my shoe;

Three, four,
knock at
the door;

Five, six, pick up sticks;

Seven, eight, lay them straight;

Nine, ten,
a big fat hen.

Six Little Mice

Six little mice sat down to spin;
Pussy passed by and she peeped in.
"What are you doing, my little men?"
"Weaving coats for gentlemen."
"Shall I come in and cut off your threads?"
"No, no, Mistress Pussy, you'd bite off our heads."
"Oh, no, I'll not, I'll help you to spin."
"That may be so, but you don't come in!"

Hot Cross Buns!

Hot cross buns! Hot cross buns!
One a penny, two a penny,
Hot cross buns!

Give them to your daughters,
Give them to your sons,
One a penny, two a penny,
Hot cross buns!

Three Little Kittens

Three little kittens, they lost their mittens,
And they began to cry,
"Oh, Mother dear, we sadly fear,
That we have lost our mittens."
"What! Lost your mittens,
you naughty kittens!
Then you shall have no pie.
Mee-ow, mee-ow, mee-ow.
Then you shall have no pie."

Three little kittens, they found their mittens,
And they began to cry,
"Oh, mother dear, see here, see here,
For we have found our mittens."
"Put on your mittens, you silly kittens!
And you shall have some pie."

Hickety Pickety

Hickety pickety, my black hen,
She lays eggs for gentlemen.
Sometimes nine and sometimes ten,
Hickety pickety, my black hen.

Two Cats of Kilkenny

There once were two cats of Kilkenny,
Each thought there was one cat too many,
So they fought and they fit,
And they scratched and they bit,
Till, excepting their nails
And the tips of their tails,
Instead of two cats, there weren't any.

One for Sorrow

One for sorrow,
Two for joy,
Three for a girl,
Four for a boy.
Five for silver,
Six for gold,

Seven for a secret,
Never to be told.
Eight for a wish,
Nine for a kiss,
Ten for a bird you
want to miss.

Three Blind Mice

Three blind mice, three blind mice,
See how they run! See how they run!
They all ran after the farmer's wife
Who cut off their tails
with a carving knife;
Did you ever see
such a thing in your life
As three blind mice?

I Love Sixpence

I love sixpence, pretty little sixpence,
I love sixpence better than my life;
I spent a penny of it, I spent another,
And I took fourpence home to my wife.

Oh, my little fourpence,
pretty little fourpence,
I love fourpence better than my life;
I spent a penny of it, I spent another,
And I took twopence home to my wife.

Oh, my little twopence,
pretty little twopence,
I love twopence better than my life;
I spent a penny of it, I spent another,
And I took nothing home to my wife.

Five Little Pussy Cats

Five little pussy cats playing near the door;
One ran and hid inside
And then there
were four.

Four little pussy cats
underneath a tree;
One heard a dog bark
And then there were three.

Three little pussy cats
thinking what to do;
One saw a little bird
And then there were two.

Two little pussy cats sitting in the sun;
One ran to catch his tail
And then there was one.

One little pussy cat looking for some fun;
He saw a butterfly
And then there was none.

It rains on the umbrellas here

WHATEVER THE WEATHER

The wind is passing through

And we shall have snow

Incy Wincy Spider

Incy Wincy Spider
Climbed up the water spout;
Down came the rain
And washed the spider out.

Out came the sun
And dried up all the rain;
So Incy Wincy Spider
Climbed up the spout again.

The Mulberry Bush

Here we go round the mulberry bush,
The mulberry bush, the mulberry bush,
Here we go round the mulberry bush,
On a cold and frosty morning.

This is the way we wash our hands,
Wash our hands, wash our hands,
This is the way we wash our hands,
On a cold and frosty morning.

This is the way we brush our hair,
Brush our hair, brush our hair,
This is the way we brush our hair,
On a cold and frosty morning.

This is the way we go to school,
Go to school, go to school,
This is the way we go to school,
On a cold and frosty morning.

This is the way we wave goodbye,
Wave goodbye, wave goodbye,
This is the way we wave goodbye,
On a cold and frosty morning.

It's Raining

It's raining, it's pouring,
The old man is snoring;
He went to bed
And bumped his head
And couldn't get up in the morning!

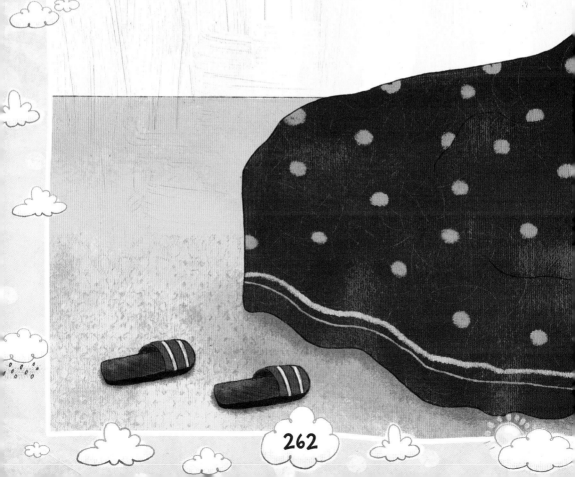

Blow, Wind, Blow

Blow, wind, blow,
And go, mill, go;
That the miller
May grind his corn;
That the baker may take it,
And into bread make it,
And bring us some
Hot in the morn.

Doctor Foster

Doctor Foster
Went to Gloucester
In a shower of rain.
He stepped in a puddle
Right up to his middle
And never went there again!

The Twelve Months

Snowy,

Flowy,

Blowy,

Showery,

Flowery,

Bowery,

Hoppy,
Croppy,
Droppy,

Breezy,
Sneezy,
Freezy.

George Ellis
1753–1815, b. England

Rain

Rain on the green grass,
Rain on the trees,
Rain on the rooftop,
But not on me!

The North Wind doth Blow

The north wind doth blow,
And we shall have snow,
And what will poor robin do then,
Poor thing?

He'll sit in a barn,
And keep himself warm,
And hide his head under his wing,
Poor thing.

Whether the Weather

Whether the weather be fine,
Or whether the weather be not,
Whether the weather be cold,
Or whether the weather be hot,
We'll weather the weather
Whatever the weather,
Whether we like it or not!

First Day of May

The fair maid who, the first of May,
Goes to the fields at break of day,
And washes in dew from the hawthorn tree,
Will ever after handsome be.

Rain

The rain is falling all around,
It falls on field and tree,
It rains on the umbrellas here,
And on the ships at sea.

Robert Louis Stevenson
1850–94, b. Scotland

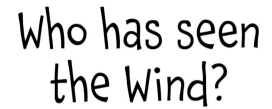

Who has seen the Wind?

Who has seen the wind?
Neither I nor you:
But when the leaves hang trembling,
The wind is passing through.

Who has seen the wind?
Neither you nor I:
But when the trees bow down their heads,
The wind is passing by.

Christina Rossetti
1830–94, b. England

Over the Hills

Tom, he was a piper's son,
He learned to play when he was young,
And all the tunes that he could play
Was, "Over the hills and far away".
Over the hills and a great way off,
The wind shall blow my top-knot off.

Rain, Rain

Rain, rain, go away,
Come again another day.

Rain, rain, go away,
Little Johnny wants to play.

Red Sky at Night

Red sky at night,
Shepherd's delight:
Red sky in the morning,
Shepherd's warning.

upstairs and downstairs
In his night gown

BEDTIME RHYMES

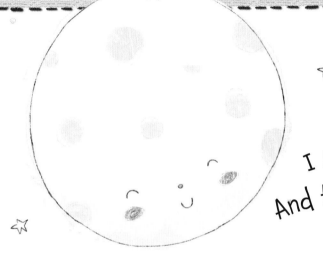

I see the moon
And the moon sees me

up above the world so high

Twinkle, Twinkle, Little Star

Twinkle, twinkle, little star,
How I wonder what you are.
Up above the world so high,
Like a diamond in the sky.

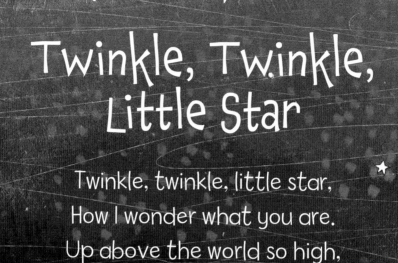

When the blazing sun is gone,
When he nothing shines upon,
Then you show your little light,
Twinkle, twinkle, all the night.

Then the traveler in the dark,
Thanks you for your tiny spark,
He could not see which way to go,
If you did not twinkle so.

In the dark blue sky you keep,
And often through my curtains peep.
For you never shut your eye,
Till the sun is in the sky.

Rock-a-bye, Baby

Rock-a-bye, baby,
On the tree-top,
When the wind blows,
The cradle will rock.

When the bough breaks,
The cradle will fall.
And down will come baby,
Cradle and all.

Come, let's to Bed

Come, let's to bed, says Sleepy-head;
Sit up awhile, says Slow;
Bang on the pot, says Greedy-gut,
We'll sup before we go.

To bed, to bed, cried Sleepy-head,
But all the rest said No!
It is morning now,
You must milk the cow,
And tomorrow to bed we go.

The Evening is Coming

The evening is coming,
The sun sinks to rest,
The birds are all flying
Straight home to the nest.

"Caw," says the crow
As he flies overhead,
"It's time little children
Were going to bed!"

Sleep, Baby, Sleep

Sleep, baby, sleep,
Thy father guards the sheep;
Thy mother shakes the dreamland tree
And from it fall sweet dreams for thee.
Sleep, baby, sleep.

Sleep, baby, sleep,
Our cottage vale is deep;
The little lamb is on the green,
The wooly fleece so soft and clean,
Sleep, baby, sleep.

Sleep, baby, sleep,
Down where the woodbines creep;
Be always like the lamb so mild,
A kind and sweet and gentle child,
Sleep, baby, sleep.

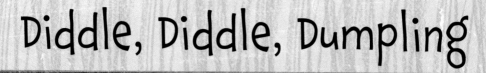

Diddle, Diddle, Dumpling

Diddle, diddle, dumpling, my son John,
Went to bed with his trousers on;
One shoe off, and one shoe on,
Diddle, diddle, dumpling, my son John.

I See the Moon

I see the moon,
And the moon sees me;
God bless the moon,
And God bless me!

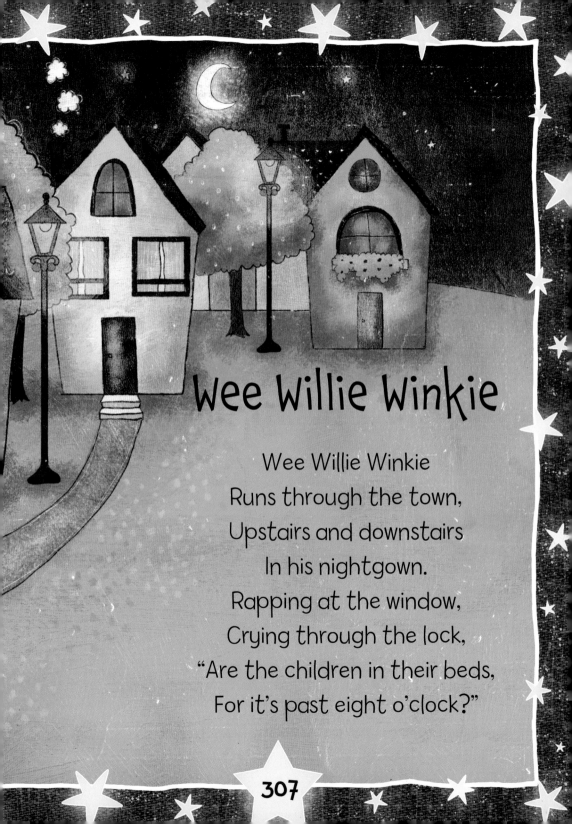

Wee Willie Winkie

Wee Willie Winkie
Runs through the town,
Upstairs and downstairs
In his nightgown.
Rapping at the window,
Crying through the lock,
"Are the children in their beds,
For it's past eight o'clock?"

Teddy Bear, Teddy Bear

Teddy bear, teddy bear, touch the ground.
Teddy bear, teddy bear, turn around.
Teddy bear, teddy bear, show your shoe.
Teddy bear, teddy bear, that will do.

Teddy bear, teddy bear, run upstairs.
Teddy bear, teddy bear, say your prayers.
Teddy bear, teddy bear, blow out the light.
Teddy bear, teddy bear, say goodnight.

Hush, Little Baby

Hush, little baby, don't say a word,
Papa's going to buy you a mocking bird.

If the mocking bird won't sing,
Papa's going to buy you a diamond ring.

If the diamond ring turns to brass,
Papa's going to buy you a looking-glass.

If the looking-glass gets broke,
Papa's going to buy you a billy-goat.

If the billy-goat runs away,
Papa's going to buy you another today.

Girls and Boys, Come Out to Play

Girls and boys, come out to play,
The moon doth shine as bright as day;
Leave your supper, and leave your sleep,
And come with your playfellows into
the street.

Come with a whoop, come with a call,
Come with a good will or not at all;
Up the ladder and down the wall,
A half-penny roll will serve us all.

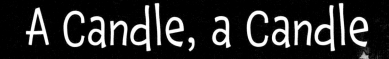

A Candle, a Candle

A candle, a candle to light me to bed;
A pillow, a pillow to tuck up my head.
The moon is as sleepy as sleepy can be,
The stars are all pointing their fingers at me.

And Missus Hop-Robin, way up in her nest,
Is rocking her tired little babies to rest.
So give me a blanket to tuck up my toes,
And a little soft pillow to snuggle my nose.

Star Light, Star Bright

Star light, star bright,
First star I see tonight.
I wish I may,
I wish I might,
Have the wish
I wish tonight.

316

The Man in
the Moon

The man in the moon
Looked out of the moon ,
And this is what he said,
"Tis time that now I'm getting up,
All babies went to bed."

Your wish will be granted

STORY
TIME

The mice were
delighted

She placed one single pea
right in the middle

321

The Three Billy Goats Gruff

Once there lived three billy goats gruff. They loved eating grass all day long. But it had to be the sweetest, tastiest grass they could find.

"Time to look for some tastier grass," said the big billy goat gruff to his brothers one day.

So they set off along the river.

They wandered for miles and miles. "Are we there yet?" asked the littlest billy goat gruff. "I'm starving hungry!"

At last they came to a bridge, and on the other side of it they saw a lush meadow. "That looks delicious!" said the littlest billy goat gruff. "Yummy!" agreed his two brothers.

But a nasty troll lived under the bridge. He had long, sharp claws, pointed teeth, and liked nothing better than goat to eat for dinner.

"I'll cross first," said the littlest billy goat gruff. And off he trotted with a trip trap, trip trap, over the wooden bridge.

Suddenly the troll jumped out in front of him. "Who is that trip-trapping over my bridge?" he roared.

"Only me," said the littlest billy goat gruff. "I need to get to the meadow beyond."

"Stop!" growled the troll. "I'm going to eat you for my dinner!"

"Oh, but you should wait until my brother comes along," said the littlest billy goat gruff. "He's

FAR bigger than me. Byeee!"
And with a hop and a skip, the
little goat jumped into the
meadow beyond.

Soon after, the middle-sized
billy goat gruff crossed the
bridge. Trip trap, trip trap!

"STOP RIGHT THERE!" the troll
roared, jumping out. "Who is
trip-trapping over MY BRIDGE?"

"It's me, looking for tasty
grass to eat," said the middle-
sized billy goat gruff.

"But I want you for my dinner," said the troll.

"Wait for my big brother. He'll make a much better meal," said the middle-sized billy goat gruff. And he jumped past the troll.

The biggest billy goat gruff came next. He was very strong with long, sharp horns. TRIP TRAP TRIP TRAP. The big billy goat gruff clattered over the wooden bridge.

"That sounds like dinner!" said the troll.

"Who is TRIP-TRAPPING over MY BRIDGE? he roared.

"ME!" said the big billy goat gruff, coming face to face with the troll. "I'm on my way to the

329

meadow beyond."

"But I want you for my dinner," said the troll a little nervously.

"I don't think so!" said the big billy goat gruff with a snort.

The big billy goat gruff lowered his head and showed the troll his long, sharp horns. He took a run at the troll and... BIFF! Up went the troll high into the air, over the

bridge and far into the river below. "ARGGGH!" shouted the troll.

TRIP TRAP, TRIP TRAP! The big billy goat gruff clattered over the bridge and jumped into the meadow beyond.

The three billy goats gruff lived happily ever after – and they were never bothered by the troll again!

Snow White and the Seven Dwarfs

One winter's day, a baby girl was born to a king and queen. She was very pretty, with skin as white as snow and lips as red as blood. The girl was named Snow White before her mother sadly died.

The king remarried, but his new queen was unkind and vain. She had a magic mirror, to which she would say, "Mirror, mirror, on the wall, who is the fairest of them all?"

"You, O queen are the fairest of them all!" it would reply.

Many years later, when Snow White was sixteen, the queen asked this same question, and the mirror replied: "Snow White is now the fairest."

The queen was furious! She
ordered a huntsman to find her
stepdaughter and kill her.

The huntsman took Snow White into the forest, but he could not bring himself to do the wicked deed. Instead, he told Snow White to flee, and went back to the queen, pretending he had carried out her wishes.

Snow White ran until evening began

to fall, when she stumbled
across a little cottage.

She walked up the path and
tried the door, and it opened.
She went inside the cottage to
see if anyone was there
– everything inside was
very small and neat.

Against the wall stood seven little beds. Snow White sank down on one and slept.

Later that night the seven dwarfs who owned the cottage came back. They had been mining for jewels.

When Snow White awoke she explained what had happened. The dwarfs said that she could stay, and look after the cottage. Each day they would say, "Be careful and don't

let anyone into
the house."

But one day, many months later, the magic mirror told the evil queen that Snow White was in fact still alive and well:

"You, O queen, are very fair – but Snow white is living with the seven dwarfs in the forest – and she is the fairest of them all."

The queen was

furious! She set out to look for Snow White that very day, disguised as an old woman. She took with her an apple that was poisoned on one side.

Eventually, after a long search through the forest, the queen found the dwarfs' cottage.

She called out to Snow White, who was inside cooking a delicious dinner for the dwarfs.

"I have apples for sale! Delicious, juicy, sweet apples!"

"No, thank you," said Snow White, but the queen wouldn't take no for an answer. She cut off a piece from the green half of the apple. "Look, I will eat some first. It is quite safe."

Snow White was very hungry, so she took the apple, taking a bite from the rosy-red side.

Straight away she fell down as if dead.
When the dwarfs came home later that day and found Snow White, they hugged each other and wept.
They made a glass coffin for Snow White near to the cottage.

Strangely, Snow White always looked as if she had just fallen into a deep sleep.

One day, a prince came riding

past. He stopped to look at Snow White, but as he leant closer he knocked the coffin. The poisoned apple fell from her

mouth and she awoke!

The prince took Snow White to his palace to recover, and they soon fell in love. The prince asked Snow White to marry him, and the dwarfs were the guests of honour at the wedding.

Meanwhile, the evil queen angrily asked her mirror one last time, "And who is the fairest of them all?"

When she heard the answer "Snow White", she burst into

flames. Snow
White and the
prince, meanwhile, lived happily
ever after.

The Town Mouse and the Country Mouse

A little mouse who lived in a busy, bustling town was on a train to the country. He was going to visit his cousin. The town mouse was very excited, as he had never been to the countryside before. Meanwhile, the country mouse was getting ready for her guest.

After a long journey, the town mouse arrived. The cousins greeted each other joyfully.

The country mouse showed off her home in a tree trunk. It was simple, but warm and cosy. "It doesn't look much like my home," the town mouse said.

Once the town mouse had rested, the country mouse took him to meet the farm animals next door. They crowded round to greet him. Curious, the horse lowered his head and sniffed at the town mouse.

"Watch it!" he cried. He wasn't

keen on these
new animals.
That evening,
the country

351

mouse served what she thought was a delicious dinner of bread and cheese. It was not at all like the fancy meals the town mouse was used to. All night, the town mouse tossed and turned in his bed of leaves. He was used to

sleeping in a much softer bed.

"How do you put up with this?" the town mouse asked in the morning. "Your food is plain and you sleep on leaves! Come to the town with me and I'll show you how to live."

The country mouse was eager to see the town, so she agreed.

The town mouse lived in a very grand house in the middle of the town. The country mouse was amazed! Inside, the town

mouse proudly showed off his home. It was very comfortable. "Let me show you the rest of the house," he said to his cousin. In the kitchen, they spotted a cat prowling around.

"Hide!" the town mouse

whispered.

They scurried under a cup. Here they waited, hardly daring to breathe. At last, the cat stalked away. "That was close!" exclaimed the country mouse.

Next, they crept into the

living room. There were people there, watching a bright, glowing screen. The country mouse gazed at it – she had never seen anything like it!

In the playroom, there were all kinds of toys. The country mouse knocked over a tower of building blocks, which came tumbling down. CRASH!

They then went to the dining room. On the table, they found a delicious-looking feast of sandwiches and pies, cakes and biscuits – everything that was good to eat. The mice helped themselves.

"I've never had food like this before!" said the country mouse.

"This is how you could eat all the time!" he replied.

Suddenly, the mice heard growling and scratching at the

door. Two dogs burst in, sniffing the air. They began to bark, jumping up at the table and the mice scampered away.

Enough was enough. The country mouse said goodbye and left for home. "Better to live poorly in peace than richly in fear," she said.

Cinderella

Once upon a time, there was a young girl called Cinderella. She lived with her mean stepmother and two stepsisters. She worked hard all day long and at night slept by the fireside, in the ashes.

One day, a letter arrived from the palace. The prince was holding a ball, and everyone was invited. Cinderella's stepmother said to her, "You cannot go. You must stay here and mind the fires."

On the day of the ball, Cinderella helped her stepsisters get ready. "Have fun at home!" they teased. Poor Cinderella watched the carriage drive away into the distance, then sat down, almost in tears.

"How I wish I could go to the ball," she said.

Suddenly, a kind-looking old lady appeared. She had glittery wings and a wand.

"Hello Cinderella," she said. "I'm your fairy godmother. I will grant your wish. You shall go to the ball after all!"

Cinderella's fairy godmother

smiled and said, "first we need a way to get you to the palace. Fetch the largest pumpkin from the vegetable patch."

She waved her wand and the

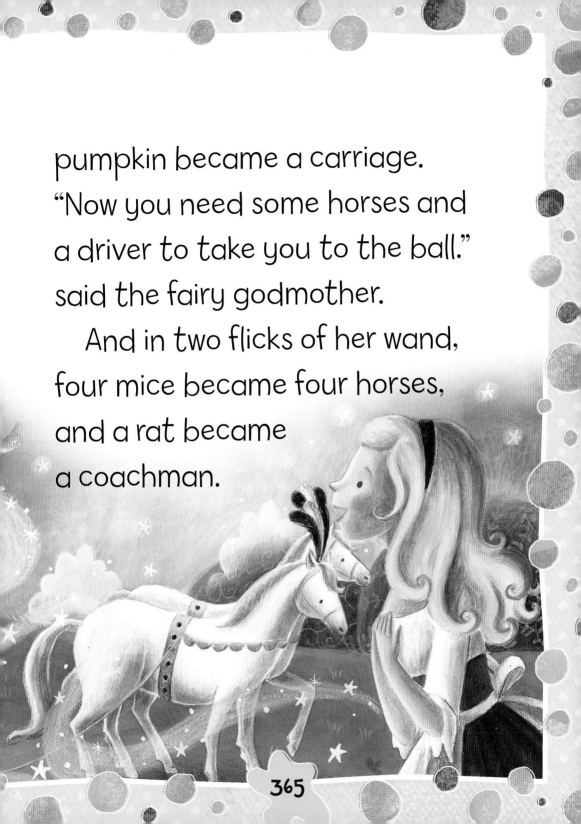

pumpkin became a carriage.
"Now you need some horses and
a driver to take you to the ball."
said the fairy godmother.

And in two flicks of her wand,
four mice became four horses,
and a rat became
a coachman.

"Now for the most important part," said Cinderella's fairy godmother, "your gown."

She twirled her wand, and when Cinderella looked down she was wearing a beautiful dress, and sparkling glass slippers.

Cinderella's fairy godmother said she was ready for the ball, but that she must be home by midnight. "The spell will end as the clock strikes twelve."

When Cinderella arrived at the

palace everyone turned to look at her. "Who is that?" they asked. Nobody recognized her, not even her stepsisters.

The prince danced with Cinderella all evening. She was enjoying herself so much that she didn't notice the time.

Suddenly the clock began to strike twelve! Cinderella ran from the palace but in her haste she lost one of her glass slippers.

Cinderella returned to her carriage but it was gone – the spell had broken. She ran home as quickly as she could. The prince, meanwhile, could not forget Cinderella — he had declared that he would marry the owner of the glass slipper.

The next day he began visiting every house in the land. The prince had no luck until he arrived at Cinderella's

house. "This glass slipper belongs to

the girl I danced with," the prince said, "I must find her."

Cinderella's stepsisters invited the prince inside, then they tried to force their big feet into the slipper, but with no luck! The prince asked if there were any other young ladies at the house.

"Of course not," said the stepsisters.

Just then, Cinderella stepped into the room, but before she could speak her stepmother said, "No, not her, she works in the kitchen – she didn't go to the ball."

But the prince asked Cinderella to sit down on the chair. She placed her foot in the glass slipper and it fitted perfectly!

Suddenly, the prince recognized Cinderella as the girl from the ball, and he was overjoyed!

"I have found my bride at long last," the prince cried. "Will you marry me?"

Cinderella said yes, and they lived happily ever after.

Chicken Licken

One fine day Chicken Licken went for a walk in the woods. Now Chicken Licken was not very bright, and he was also rather inclined to act first and think after. So when an acorn fell on his head, he decided immediately that the sky must be falling in. He set off as fast as he could to tell the king, and on the way he met Henny Penny and Cocky Locky.

"I am off to tell the king that the sky is falling in," he clucked.

"We will come too," said Henny Penny and Cocky Locky.

So Chicken Licken, Henny Penny and Cocky Locky set off to tell the king. On the way they met Ducky Lucky and Drakey Lakey.

"We are off to tell the king that the sky is falling in," clucked Chicken Licken importantly.

"We will come too," said Ducky Lucky and Drakey Lakey.

So Chicken Licken, Henny

Penny, Cocky Locky, Ducky Lucky and Drakey Lakey all set off to tell the king. On the way they met Goosey Loosey and Turkey Lurkey.

"We are off to tell the king that the sky is falling in," clucked Chicken Licken importantly.

"We will come too," said Goosey Loosey and Turkey Lurkey.

So Chicken Licken, Henny Penny, Cocky Locky, Ducky

Lucky, Drakey Lakey, Goosey Loosey and Turkey Lurkey all set off to tell the king. On the way they met Foxy Loxy.

"We are off to tell the king that the sky is falling in," clucked Chicken Licken importantly.

"What a good thing I met you all," said Foxy Loxy with a cunning smile. "I know the quickest way, follow me."

So Chicken Licken, Henny

Penny, Cocky Locky, Ducky
Lucky, Drakey Lakey, Goosey
Loosey and Turkey Lurkey all
set off behind Foxy Loxy.
He led them all straight

to his den where he ate every single one of them for his dinner!

So the king never heard that the sky was falling in (it didn't, of course).

The Little Mermaid

Deep beneath the ocean, where the water is emerald blue, lived the Sea King – a merman – and all his subjects. He lived with his daughters, the sea princesses, in a beautiful castle made of coral, shells and pearls.

The youngest mermaid was much quieter than her sisters and longed for the world above the waves. She could often be found gazing at a statue of a man that had fallen to the sea floor from a wreck, or at the water's surface sitting on a rock to watch the great ships pass by.

One night, a large ship with three masts lay on the water.

There was music and song on board and as night fell, lanterns were lit. The little mermaid swam closer to get a better look at the people onboard. Inside was a young prince. He was having a birthday party.

But all of a sudden a raging storm was upon them. The ship groaned and creaked as the waves broke over the deck — everyone was in grave danger.

The little mermaid saw the prince slip into the water. Rising and falling with the waves, she reached him, and dragged him

to the surface. The little
mermaid swam through the
night to find land, and
found a bay near a
castle. She pushed the

prince onto the warm, dry sand.
Suddenly a princess appeared
from the castle and hurried
towards the prince. The little
mermaid hid behind some rocks,
and watched from the water as

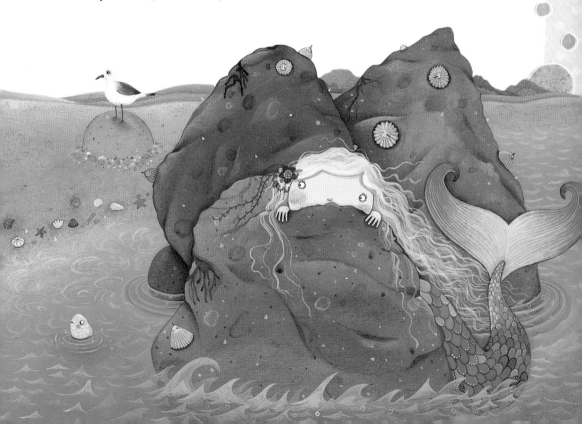

the princess helped the prince back to her father's castle to get better. They soon fell in love, although the prince couldn't help but wonder who had saved him that night.

One day soon after, a great party was held at the Sea King's palace. Everyone was dancing and singing – all apart from the little mermaid. She was longing to see her prince again.

The little mermaid left to find

the old sea
witch, who
smiled nastily
when she

asked for legs to replace her tail. "Drink this magic potion and your wish will be granted – but if the prince marries anyone

else, you must return to the sea
and become foam on the waves.
And as payment, you will lose
your voice!" she added, with an
evil, cackling laugh.

The little mermaid agreed,
as she loved the prince so
desperately. She swam to the
shore and drank
the potion. At
once, her tail
became two legs.
The little

mermaid tried to find the prince but found it very hard to walk.

After a while, the little mermaid sat down to rest and soon fell fast asleep. When she awoke, the prince was there.

"Don't worry. I'll take care of you," he said. But the little mermaid couldn't reply.

They spent lots of time together and the little mermaid fell even more in love – she liked to listen to the prince talk, even

though she couldn't reply. But
he was engaged to be married
to the princess who had found

him on the shore.

On the day of the prince's wedding the little mermaid was very sad indeed.

She left the ceremony to return to the sea, but she did not turn to foam as the witch had said. Instead, she found herself being lifted out of the water by beautiful spirits.

"Don't be sad. Come with us!" they cried. "We fly around the world to do good deeds!"

And so the little mermaid rose up to join them and was happy at long last.

Puss in Boots

There was once a miller who had three sons. When he died, he left the mill to his eldest son and a donkey to his middle son. The youngest son was given the miller's cat.

"What am I to do with a cat?" he said. Imagine his surprise when Puss replied, "Give me boots and a bag and you'll see!"

So the youngest son gave
Puss some boots and a bag. The
cat went to a field and put
carrots in the bag, then he hid
in the grass. Before long, a

rabbit hopped into the bag, tempted by the carrots. Off Puss ran to the palace, where he offered the rabbit to the king as a gift from the Marquis of Carabas. The king was delighted.

The next day, Puss said to the miller's son, "Come to the river and help me fish." Puss knew the king would be driving by. "Quick, get into the water!" said Puss. The miller's son did, just as the carriage passed by.

Then Puss hid his
master's clothes.
"STOP!" cried Puss,
and he ran in front

of the carriage to make it stop. "My master, the Marquis of

Carabas, has been robbed! Thieves stole his clothes as he swam in the river!"

The king ordered fine clothes to be brought for the miller's son. Then he was invited to ride in the carriage with the king and the princess.

In the meantime, Puss ran ahead of the carriage. He met some workers gathering hay in the fields. "When the king's carriage drives by, the king will ask who owns this land," said Puss. "Say it belongs to the Marquis of Carabas." Sure enough, this is what happened. The king was impressed.

Once again, Puss ran ahead. He came to a big castle where an ogre lived. Puss knocked loudly at the gate and a servant let him in. Puss was taken to meet the ogre, and he bowed down low. "What do you want?" the ogre growled.

Puss was scared, but he said, "I've heard you can do amazing magic Mr Ogre, and can turn yourself into any animal. But can you turn into a lion?"

The ogre immediately became a roaring lion. "It must be easy to turn into a big animal," said Puss. "I'm sure you couldn't turn into a small one... Like a mouse." So the outraged

ogre did just that. Puss seized his chance and POUNCED!

That was the end of the ogre. The servants in the castle were very happy – they had been under the ogre's spell. Pleased to be free, they agreed to become servants of the Marquis of Carabas.

Suddenly, Puss heard the king's carriage approach.

"Quick! Prepare a feast for the king and the Marquis of Carabas!" he said.

The carriage stopped and the king stepped out, amazed. "Welcome to the castle of the Marquis of Carabas!" said Puss, bowing low.

They all sat down to a huge feast that had been prepared by the servants. Soon, the king noticed that the miller's son and the princess had fallen in love.

He offered the Marquis of
Carabas his daughter's hand in

marriage and soon the princess and the miller's son were wed in a grand ceremony.

Meanwhile Puss was very pleased at the way his plan had worked out!

The Princess and the Pea

The prince was very fed up. Everyone in the court seemed to think he should be married, but he insisted that his new bride be a real, true princess – not just anyone.

He had met lots of nice girls who had said they were princesses. But, it seemed to

the prince,
either their
manners were not
good enough, or
their feet were too big.

The prince sat in the palace feeling glum, until one night there was a terrible storm. Rain lashed down, thunder rolled and lightning flashed.

Suddenly there was a knocking at the door, and there, dripping wet, stood a girl. She said she was a princess, but she didn't look like one. Her hair was plastered to her head, her dress was wringing wet and her shoes were covered in mud.

They invited
the girl in to
be polite,
but the
queen

didn't believe that she was a real princess.

While the girl sat sipping a mug of warm milk and honey, the queen supervised the making up of the bed in the second-best spare bedroom.

The queen told the maids to take off all the bedclothes and the mattress. Then she placed one single pea right in the middle of the bedstead.

Next, the maids piled twenty

mattresses on top of the pea, and then twenty feather quilts on top of the mattresses.

And so the girl was shown to the room, and left for the night.

Next morning,
the queen asked
the girl how she
had slept.

"I didn't sleep a wink all night," said the girl. "There was a great, hard lump in the middle of the bed. It was quite dreadful. I am sure I am bruised all over!"

When the queen heard her answer she knew that the girl really must be telling the truth, for only a real princess could be bruised by a tiny pea.

The prince was delighted when he heard the news! He threw his arms up in the air and went to ask the princess to marry him. Of course she said yes, for she had fallen in love with the prince, and they lived happily ever after.

As for the pea, it was placed in the museum, where it probably still is today.

Jack and the Beanstalk

This is the story of how Jack did a silly thing, but all was well in the end.

Jack and his mother were very poor, and one day Jack's mother told him to take their only cow to market, and sell her for as much money as he could possibly get.

On the way to market, Jack met a funny little man who offered him five magic beans in exchange for the cow.

Jack should have realized that this was rather odd, but he took the beans, handed over the cow and ran home.

Jack's mother was so furious she flung the beans out of the window and sent Jack straight to bed.

The next morning, Jack wandered outside to find his mother staring in amazement at an enormous beanstalk. It reached right up into the clouds. "I told you they were magic beans," said Jack, and he began to climb.

Jack climbed and climbed. At the top of the beanstalk was a huge castle. Jack knocked on the door, and a gigantic woman opened it.

"My husband eats boys for breakfast," she said. Before Jack could reply, the ground started to shake, so she hid Jack in a large cupboard.

A huge man stumped into the kitchen. "Fee fi fo fum! I smell the blood of an Englishman!" he roared loudly.

"Don't be silly, dear. You can smell the eggs I've cooked," said the giant's wife.

The giant gobbled up the

whole pile of eggs. Then, he
poured a bag of gold onto the
table, counted all the coins
and fell asleep.

Jack darted out of the
cupboard, grabbed
the bag of gold
and slithered
down the
beanstalk as fast
as he could.

Jack's
mother was

astonished when she saw the gold. They bought two new cows and plenty of food to eat.

But after a time, Jack decided to climb the beanstalk again. The giant's wife wasn't very pleased to see him.

"We lost a bag of gold the last time you were here," she growled. Then the ground began to shake and tremble. Jack ran and hid in the cupboard.

"Fee fi fo fum! I smell the blood

of an Englishman!" the enormous giant roared.

"Don't be silly, dear. You can smell the chickens I've cooked," said the giant's wife, handing him a plate.

The giant gobbled the lot. Then he lifted a tiny white goose onto the table. "Lay!" he commanded, and the goose laid a golden egg. With a smile, the giant fell asleep.

Jack darted out of the

cupboard, grabbed the goose and slid down the beanstalk.

Jack's mother was amazed when she saw the golden eggs. This time they bought a whole herd of cows.

After a while, Jack climbed the beanstalk again. The giant's wife looked very cross.

"We lost a golden goose last time you were here," she growled. Then the ground began to shake – Jack hid in a drawer.

"Fee fi fo fum! I smell the blood of an Englishman!" roared the giant.

"Try the cupboard," said the giant's wife, but this time Jack wasn't in there.

"Well, eat your breakfast," said the giant's wife, handing him a plate of sausages.

The giant ate the lot, then he lifted a harp onto the table.

"Play!" he commanded. The harp played so sweetly that the giant was soon asleep.

Jack crept out from the drawer and grabbed the golden harp. But the harp stopped playing when Jack touched it.

The giant woke up with a start and ran after Jack, who climbed down the beanstalk as fast he could, still carrying the harp under his arm.

As soon as Jack reached the ground he ran to fetch an axe and called for his mother.

Together they worked away and chopped through the giant beanstalk. After a time, down tumbled the huge beanstalk, and down tumbled the giant along with it. And that was the end of him!

So, Jack and his mother lived happily for the rest of their

days with a whole herd of cows, the little white goose and the golden harp.

Sleeping Beauty

Once upon a time a beautiful baby girl was born to a king and queen. They had wanted a child for a long time, so they were very happy.

The proud king soon began organizing a christening feast for his little princess. All the king's family and friends were invited to the christening. They

also asked the
fairies to come
– all apart from
one, who was

known for being mean. On the big day the guests arrived, bringing lots of lovely gifts. "Congratulations your highnesses!" they called.

The fairies lined up to give the baby princess her presents and they came forward one by one, casting spells of kindness, beauty and cleverness. The last fairy was just about to give her gift, when there was a loud noise in the courtyard.

Just then, the mean fairy who had not been invited burst in angrily, and said, "When the princess is fifteen she shall touch a spindle and fall down dead!"

The queen collapsed into the king's arms in shock, but then the last fairy stepped forward.

"Wait!" she said. "I can soften the curse a little. If the princess touches a spindle, she will not die. Instead, she will fall asleep for one hundred years. However, only a prince shall be able to wake her with a single kiss."

The king gave out an order for all the spindles in the land to be destroyed straightaway, so the

princess grew up without ever seeing one.

Over the next fifteen years, the princess grew up into a beautiful young lady, then one day she came across a strange door in the castle.

She opened it and found some steps, which lead to a tower. In the tower was a woman, busy at a strange wheel.

"Hello, what are you doing?" asked the princess.

"I'm spinning, my dear," said the woman.

The princess reached out to touch the spindle.

"Ouch!" the princess cried as her finger touched the spindle, and while the wicked fairy – for

it was she — vanished, the
princess fell down asleep.

At that moment the king and queen fell asleep on their thrones. The horses slept in their stables and the servants slipped into a slumber.

Days, weeks and then months went past, and a large hedge of thorns grew around the palace. Every year it became thicker, until the palace became hidden.

Exactly one hundred years later, a prince was riding nearby. He could see the tips of a turret above the thorns. As he neared, the hedge parted, allowing him to pass through.

The prince eventually arrived at the palace and saw that everyone and everything had been frozen in time. Finally, he came to the room where the princess was sleeping. She was so beautiful that he leant over to give her a kiss. At that moment she opened her eyes and woke up. They fell in love at first sight, and were soon happily married.

The Hare and
the Tortoise

The hare was always boasting
about how fast he could run.
"I'm the fastest animal in the
land," he would say to anyone
who would listen.

One day the hare asked,
"Who will run a race against me?
I bet I'll win!"

The other animals were fed up

with the hare's boasting, but no one would accept his challenge for fear of losing — no one except the tortoise.

"Ha ha!" The hare laughed out loud. The other animals gasped but the tortoise just smiled.

Preparations for the race began. The fox drew up a map of the route. The race was to take place the following week.

For the next seven days the hare showed off, speeding

around the meadow, dashing up hills, knocking animals over and upsetting just about everyone.

The tortoise just watched from afar as he chewed leisurely on grass and leaves.

The night before the race, the

tortoise went to bed
early, smiling happily
as the sun went down.
"Early to bed,
early to rise,"

he said to himself. Meanwhile, the hare stayed up late, partying with his neighbours, the badgers. Their noisy antics kept everyone awake, apart from the tortoise.

The next day dawned bright and sunny. The tortoise awoke refreshed and full of energy. He ate a hearty breakfast then got ready for the race.

The hare wasn't feeling quite so refreshed. His late night

meant he had hardly slept.

He poured himself a large glass of carrot juice and yawned loudly, while out in the meadow, the animals were gathering to watch the race. There were stalls selling cakes and sandwiches and balloons and bunting had been tied to trees. A party atmosphere was building!

At last it was time for the race to start. Feeling more like his usual self, the hare took his place at the start line.

"Get ready to lose!" he said to the tortoise.

The tortoise just
smiled. He didn't seem worried
at all. Then the fox began the
countdown to the race.

"On your marks... Get set..."

The whistle blew, and they were off! The hare dashed away at full speed, around the meadow then up the hill. He stopped to look back and saw the tortoise plodding along far behind.

Grinning happily, the hare danced a little jig on the hilltop. The sun was warm and he decided to have a short nap. After all, he'd had a late night, and the tortoise was far behind.

In the meantime, the tortoise carried on, up the hill and over the top. He saw the hare snoozing under a tree, and marched bravely past.

Much, much later, feeling stiff and cold, the hare woke up with a start. He looked up at the sun and saw how low it was in the sky. It must be almost evening! He feared the worst and flew around the rest of the route at top speed.

But in the distance he heard shouting and clapping, and could just make out the tortoise nearing the finish line.

With the finish line in sight, the tortoise staggered on as fast as he could. A few minutes later he crossed the line to huge applause and the crowd shouting his name – the hare had lost his own challenge. From now on perhaps he wouldn't be so boastful. The tortoise had shown the hare that slow and steady wins the race.

The Three Little Pigs

Once there were three little pigs. They lived happily with their mother until the day came for them to make their own way in the world.

"Goodbye Mum!" said the three little pigs.

They hadn't gone far when the three little pigs decided to

stop for a picnic. "Where are we going to live?" the little girl pig asked her brothers.

Then one of the little boy pigs saw a farmer with a cartload full of straw.

"Perfect house-building material," said the little pig, and he bought the whole load.

The little pig soon built his straw house. Suddenly he heard a voice outside say, "Let me in little pig!" It was a hungry wolf.

"Not by the hair on my chinny chin chin!" replied the little pig.

"Then I'll huff and I'll puff and I'll BLOW your house down!"

The wolf blew down the house of straw, but the little pig

managed to escape.

The two other little pigs carried on their way, until they met a woman with a huge load of sticks. The second little boy pig bought the sticks and built a house. Then along came the big bad wolf. He knocked on the door of the stick house.

"Let me in little pig, let me in!" But the second little pig called out, "Not by the hair on my chinny chin chin!"

"Then I'll huff and I'll puff and I'll BLOW your house down!"

And the house of sticks was

blown down! The second little pig made his getaway. He ran off as quickly as he could to find his brother and sister.

Now, the little girl pig had

bought a load of bricks, and set about building a strong, sturdy house. She worked very hard, and soon the house was ready.

The little pig was very pleased with herself and she quickly settled into her new home. But soon there was a knock at the door. It was her brothers! The boy pigs told their sister about the big bad wolf and they came up with a plan to stop him.

Soon there was another knock at the door. The third little pig peeked out of the window to see who it was. It was the big bad wolf.

"Little pig, let me in!"

"Not by the hair on my chinny chin chin!" the third little pig called out.

"Then I'll huff and I'll puff and

I'll BLOW your house down!"

The wolf huffed and puffed, and puffed and huffed. But the brick house was too strong for the wolf to blow down.

Inside, the little pigs put a

pot of water on the fire.

The wolf climbed onto the roof and down the chimney, but the pot of water was bubbling away. Suddenly there was a SPLASH! as the wolf fell into the pot. "The big bad wolf is dead at last!" the three little pigs cried.

And they all lived happily ever after in the house of bricks.

Little Red Riding Hood

Little Red Riding Hood lived in a cottage by a wood. One day her mother said, "Your Grandma is feeling ill. Please take this basket of cakes and fruit to her."

So Little Red Riding Hood set off, wearing her red cape. "Make sure you don't talk to strangers!

Especially not
wolves!" her Mum
called after her.

The trees were tall and made scary shadows. Suddenly, a wolf jumped out.

"Hello," growled the wolf. "Where are you going?"

"I'm taking some cakes and fruit to my Grandma,"

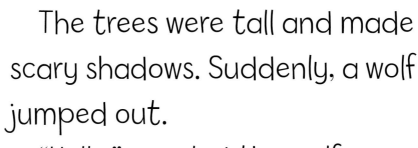

said Little Red Riding Hood.

"What a sweet child you are," said the wolf.

"Why not pick your Grandma some flowers too?"

With that the big bad wolf ran off, leaving Little Red Riding Hood happily picking flowers.

Little did she know, the wolf had raced ahead to Grandma's house, and when he arrived, the wolf knocked softly on the door.

"Let me in Grandma," he

called out. But Grandma wasn't silly. "That's not Little Red Riding Hood's voice," she said. Quickly, she hid inside the wardrobe.

"Grandma?"

The wolf burst into the cottage, but Grandma was

nowhere to be seen. So he dressed himself in her nightgown and bedcap and got into bed.

Soon, Little Red Riding Hood knocked on the door.

"Come in dear," snarled the wolf in his nicest voice.

"Grandma, you look odd!" said Little Red Riding Hood.

"Come and sit beside me dear," growled the wolf.

Little Red Riding Hood sat on the bed. "What big ears you

have Grandma," she said.
   "All the better to
hear you with, my
dear," replied
the wolf.

"What big eyes you have."

"All the better to see you with, my dear."

"And your teeth are HUGE!" said Little Red Riding Hood.

"All the better to EAT you with!" growled the wolf, and he pounced at her.

Little Red Riding Hood screamed and ran away. The wolf leapt after her, but there was a sudden banging at the door. Little Red Riding Hood flung open the door — it was a woodcutter who had heard her scream. He raised his axe. With a howl, the big bad wolf dashed out of the cottage. Grandma came out of the wardrobe,

safe at last.

Never again did Little Red Riding Hood talk to strangers. As for the wolf, he kept well away from little girls – especially those wearing red capes!

The Lion and the Mouse

There was once a lion who lived on the grassy plains, close to the edge of the jungle. Each day he roamed the grasslands, checking that all was well in his kingdom.

He feared no one,

but everyone feared him. The elephant mothers warned their babies about the lion: "Stay away from the lion. Keep your distance and all will be well."

Now when it grew too hot during the day, the lion would walk

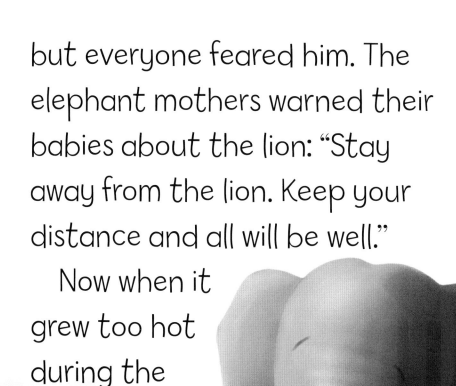

into the jungle, where the shade of the trees meant it was cool and dark. He would roam through the shady jungle until he reached his cave. Here he slept for a few hours.

A family of mice also lived in the jungle. They had a nest in a hole in a tree, and each day the young mice were sent to look for food. One of the little mice was particularly curious, and he often ventured further than his brothers and sisters.

One day, the mouse reached the edge of the jungle. He saw great plains of grass and herds of animals. He gasped at the sight of the lion on his rock, and scurried back into the jungle.

Each day, the little mouse saw the lion walking to his cave to sleep, and his curiosity got the better of him. He just had to look inside.

So one day, the mouse went to visit the lion's cave. He knew the lion was on the plains, so he crept through the jungle until he arrived at the cave.

Suddenly, a giant paw trapped the mouse – it was the lion!

"Please let me go!" begged the mouse. "I wasn't causing trouble!"

"Well you ARE in trouble!" growled the lion. "What are you doing in my cave?"

"Just being curious, Sir, but if you let me go, I promise one day to do you a good turn."

The lion laughed. "As if you could help me, king of the beasts! But you are so small, and I suppose quite brave. Be gone – and NEVER come back here again!" The mouse scampered away as fast as his legs could carry him.

Some weeks later as he prowled through the jungle, a strong net of ropes fell on

top of the lion – it was a trap! But the more he struggled to free himself, the more entangled he became. He realized the hunter would return soon. Exhausted, he lay still and roared softly.

Then the lion saw a tiny creature standing in front of him. It was the mouse. "Let me help you," squeaked the mouse, and he began gnawing the rope.

Before long, the ropes fell

away from the lion and he gave a mighty shake. "Thank you," growled the lion.

Suddenly the lion placed the mouse gently on his back. "Hold on tight to my mane," he said.

And then they were racing through the jungle. Soon they arrrived at the grassy plain.

"Meet the mouse!" called the lion to the animals. "He saved me from a trap!"

The lion had learnt that little friends may prove to be great friends.

Goldilocks and the Three Bears

Once upon a time there was a little girl called Goldilocks, who lived in a forest with her parents. Ever since she was tiny, her mother had told her not to wander off. But, one day, when her mother was busy in the kitchen, Goldilocks sneaked into the woods.

For as long as she could remember, Goldilocks had longed to explore the forest. She was happily looking at the wildflowers when she saw a little cottage between the trees. Goldilocks walked over to it, opened the door and looked inside. On a wooden table there were three bowls of steaming hot porridge – a big one, a middle-sized one and a little one.

Goldilocks was so tired and hungry that she sat down to eat the porridge.

The big bowl of porridge was too lumpy. The middle-sized bowl was far too sweet. But the little bowl was just right, so she ate it all up.

Around the fireplace were three chairs – a big one, a middle-sized one and a little one. Goldilocks couldn't climb onto the big one. The middle-sized one was too hard. The little one was just right, but as soon as she sat down, it broke into pieces!

Goldilocks suddenly felt tired so she went upstairs to find somewhere to sleep.

There, she found three beds – a big one, a middle-sized one and a little one. She tried the big bed first, but it was much too hard. The middle-sized one was too soft. But the little bed felt just right, so Goldilocks climbed in and fell fast asleep.

Now, the cottage belonged to

three bears, and when they arrived home, they soon realized someone had been inside their cottage. They noticed that the porridge bowls had been moved.

"Who has been eating my porridge?" growled Father Bear.

Mother Bear grumbled, "Who has been eating my porridge?"

And Baby Bear gasped, "Who has been eating my porridge, and has eaten it ALL up?"

Next, the bears looked at

their chairs by the fire.

Father Bear growled, "Who has been sitting on my chair?"

Mother Bear grumbled, "Who has been sitting on my chair?"

And Baby Bear gasped, "Who has been sitting on my chair,

and has BROKEN it into bits?"
Baby Bear began to cry.

Then, the bears went upstairs
to the bedroom. Father Bear
growled, "Who has been sleeping
in my bed?"

Mother Bear grumbled, "Who
has been sleeping in my bed?"

And Baby Bear gasped, "Who
has been sleeping in my bed,
AND is still there?"

Goldilocks woke up and saw
the three cross-looking bears

staring at her. She jumped out of the bed, ran downstairs and out of the door. Goldilocks ran all the way home and the three bears never saw her again.

The Boy Who Cried Wolf

There was once a shepherd boy who tended to his flock of sheep at the foot of a

mountain, near a thick forest.

He was out on the slopes all day by himself, and was often lonely and bored.

One day, the shepherd boy thought up a plan where he could get a little company and some excitement.

He left his flock unattended and rushed down the slopes to the village. He pretended to be in a terrible panic and shouted, "Wolf!" at the top of his voice.

The villagers came running to help him. But when they realized there was no wolf, they returned to their homes grumbling about the boy shouting false alarms.

A few days later the naughty boy tried the same trick again.

He ran down the mountainside shouting, "Wolf! Wolf!" Again the people came rushing to help him. This time the villagers were very angry when they realized the boy had managed to trick

509

them once more.

But just a few days later a wolf really did come out of the forest! Of course, the boy ran to

the town crying, "Wolf! Wolf!"
But the villagers, who had
already been fooled twice,
thought the boy was lying

again, so the wolf made a good meal of the boy's flock!

The shepherd boy had learnt that a liar will not be believed, even when he speaks the truth.